Who Lives in the Woods?

Written by Anne Meyers

STECK-VAUGHN
COMPANY

ELEMENTARY • SECONDARY • ADULT • LIBRARY

Who lives in the woods?
Let's take a nature walk.

2

Someone sleeps in the day and hunts at night.
Do you know who?

It's an owl.

Someone has long ears and brown fur.
Do you know who?

It's a rabbit.

Someone is brown and has a white tail.

Do you know who?

It's a deer.

Someone stores nuts in the winter.

Do you know who?

It's a chipmunk.

Someone hides in a den and is very sly.
Do you know who?

It's a fox.

Someone lives inside a cave and is very big.

Do you know who?

It's a bear.

Who else lives in the woods?

It's a forest ranger.